July Is a Mad Mosquito

ATHENEUM 1994 NEW YORK

Maxwell Macmillan Canada
Toronto

Maxwell Macmillan International
New York Oxford Singapore Sydney

July Is a Mad Mosquito

by J. Patrick Lewis

illustrated by Melanie W. Hall

Atheneum
Macmillan Publishing Company
866 Third Avenue
New York, NY 10022

Maxwell Macmillan Canada, Inc.
1200 Eglinton Avenue East
Suite 200
Don Mills, Ontario M3C 3N1

Macmillan Publishing Company is part of the Maxwell
Communication Group of Companies.

First edition
Printed in Singapore
10 9 8 7 6 5 4 3 2 1
The text of this book is set in 16-point Berkeley Old Style.
The illustrations are collagraphs.

Library of Congress Cataloging-in-Publication Data

Lewis, J. Patrick.
July is a mad mosquito / by J. Patrick Lewis; illustrated by
Melanie W. Hall.—1st ed.
p.   cm.
Summary: A poem for each month of the year evokes the sounds,
smells, and sights of the time.
ISBN 0-689-31813-8
1. Nature—Juvenile poetry.   2. Months—Juvenile poetry.
3. Children's poetry, American.   [1. Months—Poetry.   2. American
poetry.]   I. Hall, Melanie W., ill.   II. Title.
PS3562.E9465J85   1994
811'.54—dc20   93-19743

To Jim & Kate
and
Emma & Teddy
—J.P.L.

For Gurumayi,
who taught me to be at home in the heart
—M.H.

January

The snowshoe rabbit
    Sees the grouse
Hiding beside
    His snowshoe house—
A country dressed
    In winter white
Is best for keeping
    Out of sight.

Raw days like these
    No sparrow dares;
The month is made
    For polar bears
And timber wolves.
    Great days of ice!
Refrigerated
    Paradise.

SIX MORE WEEK

February

Ice-skating ponds
Begin to crack—
Old Winter's wearing thin.
It won't be long
Before the song-
Bird serenades begin.

Safely under
The weather, Mole
Sleeps at his subway stop.
His next-door neighbor's
Tunnels go
Up to the crowd on top—

Where Groundhog
Punxsutawney Phil!
Is first to spread the news:
My shadow's on
The meadow!
Six more weeks of winter blues.

March

One day this coldhearted guest
Blusters in and thumps his chest,
Bends
     the
         birches
            to
               their
                  knees,
Nips the buds off all the trees.

Chickadees, two chipper chaps,
Trimmed in coal black bibs and caps,
Hop across the heather row,
Chirping *"Tut-tut-tut!"* to snow.

                 climb!
           to
          start
         may
Temperatures
Crocuses poke up in time.
March, the bullyboy, leaves town
Once the weather settles down.

April

My windowpane,
Blue-rinsed with rain,
Looks out on new
Grass wet with dew—
Earthworms crawl plain-
Ly into view.

And unaware
Of danger there,
Two earthworms cling
To leafy spring—
Which makes a pair
Of robins sing!

May

Oh, Caterpillar, where will you hide
After tonight sets today aside?

Crab apple blossoms, a field of clover,
A buttermilk jug or the back porch swing.

Slow Caterpillar, didn't you know?
You've so little time, yet so far to go.

Ladybug Lady, before the month's over,
I'll fly away on the butterfly wing.

June

Sunny bee, Honey bee
Nectar Inspector drops
Into my garden for
Peony tea—

Sipping sweet drinks on a
Hot afternoon takes the
Sting out of summer for
Me and the bee.

July

One for the kid with the corn-dog stick
Two for his Sno-Kone sister
Three for the girl in the Dunking Booth
You tried to sink but missed her

Four for the Labrador licking the pool
Five for the mad mosquitoes
Six hurrays for the Dreamsicle days
Seven for the bee torpedoes

Eight for *ka-bang!* and *ka-boom-boom-boom!*
Nine for the fireflies dancing
Ten for the Fourth of July parade
And the Color Guard advancing

Red-hot summer days are here!
And white-hot firework nights!
Turn up the heat
And the marching beat
But don't turn out the lights!

August

At bedtime, outside
my room…nighthawk and trainsong
on the wind's guitar.

September

They've closed the public
　　Swimming pool,
And children swarm
　　Like fish to school.

The bright orange bus
　　Revs up, but boys
And girls outshout
　　The engine noise.

Late summer skies
　　Wind-whistle songs.
Dry heat heads south
　　Where it belongs—

On city streets
　　And rural routes
Where folks still wear
　　Their bathing suits.

October

When the cottonwoods sway and sigh *I wish*
And the last cider apples *ka-thunk* on the ground

The great horned owl in his crimson tree
Sees the geese V-turn in the blue goose sky

While a black cat sings to the new moon *Oh*
And a dog sees the light in a pumpkin's grin

And a batwinged boy and a witchy girl fly
Round a house on a hill going round all around

And the great horned owl in his crimson tree
Looks into the world and he calls it *Ho-ome*

November

The bottoms of autumn
Wear diamonds of frost;
The tops of the trees rue
The leaves that they've lost.

Red squirrels, busy packing
Oak cupboards for weeks,
Still rattle the branches
With seeds in their cheeks.

Gray clouds go on promising
Winter's first storm,
So we stay inside by
The stove to keep warm.

Home biscuits are baking,
The gravy is stirred,
Two pumpkin pies cool
By the thank-you bird.

December

Blue chimney smoke
Curls up and lies
Across the village square,
And people kiss by mistletoe…
There's something in the air!

The tinseled tree,
The Christmas goose,
Two carolers on the green,
Who just became a trio
With my snowman in between.

And Mother's in the kitchen
Setting out a plate of cheese
And cookies—
And eight celery sticks—
So hurry, reindeer, please!

January's a polar bear;
February's a mole,
Fast asleep and dreaming
Down a winter-dark hole.

March, the backyard robin,
Struts up to April's worm,
Staring at a feast of spring,
Daring him to squirm.

May's a monarch butterfly;
June's a thousand bees,
Violining symphonies
Under the linden trees.

July's one mad mosquito;
        Late August is a hawk,
Circling over summer and
        The summer-gone talk.

September is a school of fish;
        October's great horned owl
Eyes kindergarten goblins
        With a curious scowl.

November's the tom turkey
        We couldn't wait to roast,
But the deer that is December
        Is what I remember most.

The End